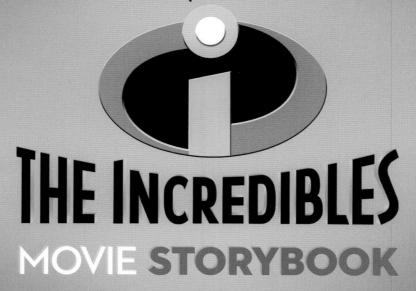

THE INCREDIBLES

MOVIE STORYBOOK

rhcbooks.com
ISBN 978-0-7364-3859-9
Printed in the United States of America
10 9 8 7 6 5 4 3 2 1

THE INCREDIBLES

Adapted by **JESSICA COLBURN**

Illustrated by the **DISNEY STORYBOOK ART TEAM**

Random House 🏠 New York

During the Golden Age of Supers, one hero stood out from the rest: **MR. INCREDIBLE**! He used his super strength to capture villains and protect innocent citizens. No one knew that under his mask and suit, Mr. Incredible was a regular citizen named Bob Parr.

There were other Supers, too. Heroes like **ELASTIGIRL**, who could stretch across vast expanses to knock out an unsuspecting bad guy; **FROZONE**, who could freeze villains instantly; and **GAZERBEAM**, whose laser-like vision sought out evildoers. Each of these crime fighters was superb. But when Mr. Incredible was on the job, he never allowed a single one to fight by his side. He didn't want to be upstaged.

Ordinary citizens idolized the Supers, but no one worshipped Mr. Incredible more than a young boy named **BUDDY**. Although he didn't have powers, Buddy wanted to be Mr. Incredible's sidekick.

One evening, Buddy showed up at a crime scene to help Mr. Incredible fight the notorious **BOMB VOYAGE**. But when Buddy wasn't looking, the villain clipped a small explosive to Buddy's cape!

Mr. Incredible was able to save Buddy, but the bomb exploded on an elevated track! The Super used his amazing strength to **STOP** an oncoming train from falling off the rails! Unfortunately, Bomb Voyage slipped away.

Mr. Incredible sent Buddy home with a police escort. "Take this one home, and make sure his mom knows what he's been doing," he said.

Buddy felt **EMBARRASSED** and **REJECTED**.

But Mr. Incredible didn't have time to dwell on that. After saving the city again, he put on a tuxedo and arrived at a church—just in time to marry Helen (also known as **ELASTIGIRL**)! All the Supers were in attendance, including **LUCIUS BEST** (better known as Frozone), who was the best man.

Bob and Helen's wedding was a glorious day during the height of the Golden Age for Supers.

However, that Golden Age was quickly coming to an end. Over the next fifteen years, Supers were attacked by **RUMORS**, **LAWSUITS**, and **NEGATIVE PRESS** coverage. They were forbidden to use their powers in public, and the Super Relocation Program was born. Its purpose was to protect the heroes by forcing them to go into hiding and live as ordinary citizens.

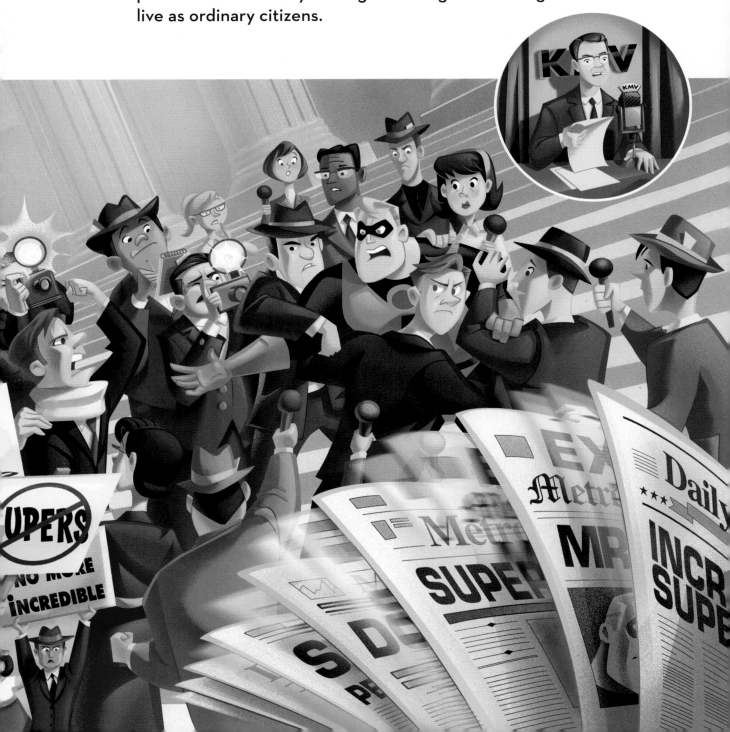

Mr. Incredible had to surrender his Superhero identity and became known as **BOB PARR**. Eventually he was hired as a clerk at an insurance company. He still helped people—but now he had to do it by filing insurance claims in a dull, cramped office.

Despite his boring job, Bob knew he had to stick with it. He had already been relocated three times since the Supers went underground. He was running out of options.

Bob's Super family was also trying to live a normal life. Bob and Helen had three kids: VIOLET, DASHIELL, and JACK-JACK. Vi and Dash were born with powers. Vi had the ability to become invisible and create force fields, and Dash had lightning speed. Baby Jack-Jack didn't appear to have any powers.

One evening during dinner, Vi and Dash began fighting. Helen stretched her arms and grabbed hold of each child while Bob LIFTED his tangled family, table and all, into the air.

Just then, the doorbell rang. It was Lucius. Bob told Helen they were going bowling and quickly left the house.

But Bob and Lucius didn't go bowling. They sat in a parked car, listening to a police scanner. Bob was itching for an excuse to be a hero and save the day.

Lucius didn't feel the same way. "To tell you the truth, I'd rather go bowling," he said.

Suddenly, they heard a report of a building on fire—with people trapped inside! Bob didn't hesitate. He charged toward the burning building with Lucius in tow.

Little did they know a **MYSTERIOUS WOMAN** was watching them.

Bob and Lucius put on ski masks to protect their identities. Then the former Supers raced into the burning building to rescue people. Nothing could stop them . . . until Lucius became **DEHYDRATED**. He couldn't use his freezing powers! Bob was forced to smash through a brick wall to escape the burning building.

Unfortunately, they wound up in a jewelry store, where they accidentally set off an alarm system. A police officer was quick to respond. **"FREEZE!"** the cop yelled.

Thankfully, Lucius was able to do just that. After sneaking a quick drink, Lucius froze the officer—buying the heroes just enough time to flee the scene.

But it had been close. Too close.

When Bob returned home that night, Helen was **WAITING** for him. She knew exactly what he'd been doing.

"Is this rubble?" she asked. "You know how I feel about that, Bob! We can't blow our cover again."

"I performed a public service. You act like that's a bad thing," said Bob.

"Uprooting our family again because you need to relive the glory days is a very bad thing!" she shouted.

The couple continued to argue, but one thing was clear: Bob just couldn't **LET GO OF THE PAST**.

The next day, Bob had a meeting with his boss, Mr. Huph. While Mr. Huph was yelling at him, Bob looked out a window and saw a person being mugged. "That man out there needs help!" he cried.

But Mr. Huph ignored him. He didn't care about other people like Bob did.

BOB LOST IT. He grabbed his boss by the collar and hurled him through **FIVE** office walls.

That was Bob's last day at Insuricare.

Without his job, Bob knew the family would have to pack up and relocate . . . again. He returned home and retreated to his den, only to discover a small tablet hidden in his briefcase.

"Hello, Mr. Incredible," said the woman onscreen. "MY NAME IS MIRAGE."

The woman explained that she represented a top-secret division of the government that was in need of Mr. Incredible's unique abilities. "If you accept, your payment will be triple your current annual salary. Rest assured, your secret is safe with us," said Mirage.

Bob was intrigued. This job would allow him to be a hero again! And for now, he wouldn't have to tell Helen he'd been fired.

The next morning, Bob told Helen he was going out of town for a work conference. Secretly, he donned his old Supersuit and boarded an ultra-sleek jet headed toward the volcanic island of Nomanisan. Mirage was on board and began briefing Mr. Incredible on his assignment.

"**THE OMNIDROID 9000** is a top-secret prototype battle robot. Its artificial intelligence enables it to solve any problem it's confronted with," Mirage began. "And unfortunately—"

"It got smart enough to wonder why it had to take orders," said Mr. Incredible. "You want me to shut it down without completely destroying it." His hero instincts were on fire.

Mirage was impressed. "You **are** Mr. Incredible," she said with a sly smile.

Moments later, Mirage escorted Mr. Incredible to the shuttle bay of the jet. He boarded a small pod and repeated his mission objectives: **"SHUT IT DOWN. DO IT QUICKLY. DON'T DESTROY IT."**

"And don't die," added Mirage.

In an instant, the pod was released and Mr. Incredible hurtled toward the island.

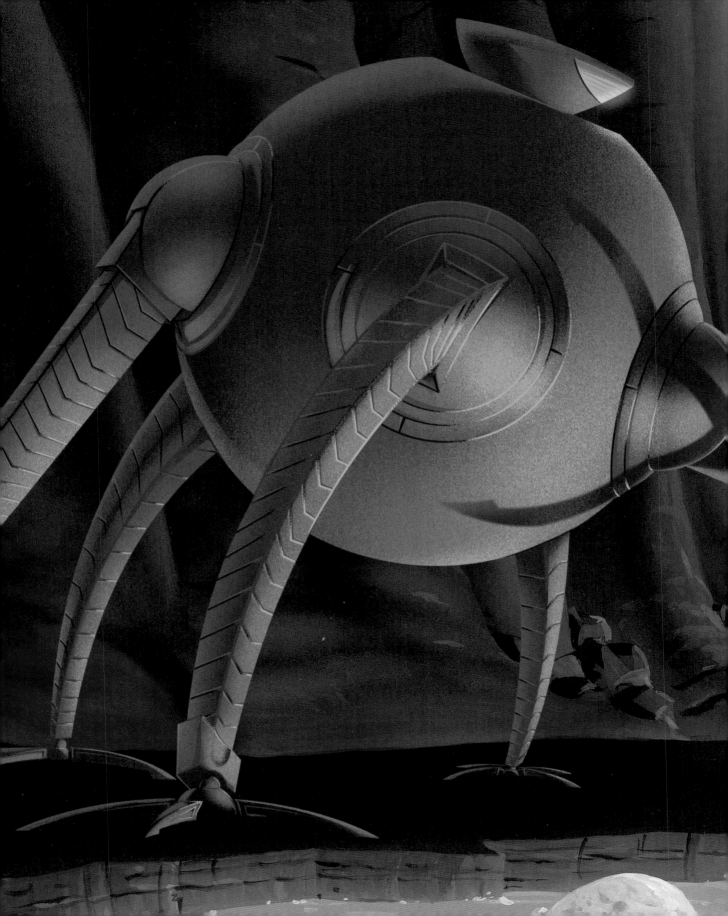

Mr. Incredible found and battled the Omnidroid, but he was **OUT OF SHAPE**. The mission was more difficult than he'd anticipated. At one point, he even tweaked his back!

Eventually Mr. Incredible figured out the Omnidroid's weakness: the robot was programmed to destroy its enemy, even if it meant destroying itself in the process. Mr. Incredible blinded the bot, then climbed inside it! The robot began to punch holes in itself as it tried to get to Mr. Incredible—until it finally collapsed.

Mr. Incredible had completed his mission. But he didn't know that Mirage had been watching him on-screen, with a mysterious man by her side.

Bob returned home **A NEW MAN**. With the money he'd made from the mission, he bought new cars for Helen and himself. He spent more time with Violet, Dash, and Jack-Jack. And the tenderness between him and Helen seemed to return.

There was just one problem: he hadn't told Helen about his Superhero work. When Bob left the house each day, he said he was headed to Insuricare, when in fact he was headed to the train yard to **GET IN SHAPE** and **BULK UP** for future missions.

One morning, Bob realized his Supersuit was torn. There was only one person who could repair it: **EDNA MODE**, or E for short. During the Golden Age of Supers, she'd been the top designer of Supersuits.

"You need a new suit!" E declared. "It will be bold. Dramatic. Heroic."

"Yeah, something classic—like Dynaguy," said Bob. "He had a great look. The cape, the boots . . ."

"NO CAPES!" exclaimed E. That was her one fashion rule.

For sentimental reasons, she also agreed to patch the tear in Bob's old suit.

It wasn't long before Mr. Incredible was back on Nomanisan Island, sporting a new suit and ready to take down another evil droid. Only this time, the droid had evolved, and it caught the Superhero off guard. As the droid's claws tightened around Mr. Incredible, a **STRANGE MAN** appeared . . . the same man who'd secretly watched him defeat the first Omnidroid.

Mr. Incredible recognized him. "Buddy?" he asked.

"My name's not Buddy . . . ," the man began. **"I'M SYNDROME! YOUR NEMESIS!"**

Sure enough, it was the kid who'd caused the Bomb Voyage fiasco years before. He was all grown up and seriously bitter toward Mr. Incredible and the rest of the Supers.

Syndrome forced Mr. Incredible into the air with his immobi-ray and tossed him over a waterfall. The villain sent a probe after Mr. Incredible to confirm his defeat.

But Mr. Incredible was hiding in a dark cave behind a skeleton, which tricked the probe's scanner into thinking he was dead.

Mr. Incredible soon learned that the skeleton belonged to **GAZERBEAM**, a former Super. He also noticed that Gazerbeam had used his laser vision to burn a word into the wall of the cave before he died. The word was **KRONOS**.

Back at home, Helen discovered the repair job on Bob's Supersuit. She raced to Edna's mansion, knowing that E was the only person Bob would have trusted with such a task.

When Helen arrived, E told her that Bob's new Supersuit had inspired her to create suits for the whole family. Helen finally realized that Bob had resumed Super work . . . and had been lying to her about it for months.

"So you don't know where he is," said E.

Helen agreed—she had no idea where Bob was.

"WOULD YOU LIKE TO FIND OUT?" E asked, handing her a remote control. E had installed a homing device in Bob's new suit. With the push of a button, Helen would know his exact location.

Meanwhile, on the island, Mr. Incredible had infiltrated Syndrome's lair and found his mainframe computer. When prompted for the password, he typed in **KRONOS** and unlocked Syndrome's enormous database. Mr. Incredible was shocked by what he discovered.

Over the last fifteen years, Syndrome had destroyed a number of Supers from the Golden Age. It was all part of his evil plan to unleash the Omnidroid in the city of Metroville and be the only "hero" who could stop it.

Mr. Incredible frantically searched the database for Helen's status: **ELASTIGIRL: LOCATION UNKNOWN.**

Mr. Incredible sighed with relief. But then he heard
beeping . . . and it was coming from his suit. It was the homing
device, which Helen had activated back at E's mansion.

Syndrome's security system was immediately triggered.
As Mr. Incredible raced for the exit, he was hit by balls of
STICKY GOO. He fell to the floor, swallowed by the expanding
slime, and lost consciousness.

After discovering Bob's location, Helen knew he was in danger. She leaped into action, took the Supersuits from E, and called in a favor for some fast transportation.

When Helen explained the situation to Vi and Dash, they **REFUSED** to be left out. They found a babysitter for Jack-Jack and snuck aboard the jet.

Vi told Helen that Dash had run away. "I thought he'd try to sneak on the plane, so I came here," she said. "It's not my fault!"

"That's not true!" yelled Dash. "This was *your* idea!"

Meanwhile, Mr. Incredible was in restraints. He'd been captured by Syndrome and Mirage.

"Who did you contact?" Syndrome asked. "You sent out a homing signal, and now a government plane is requesting permission to land here!"

Mirage played the transmission. Mr. Incredible instantly recognized his wife's voice. "Helen!" he gasped.

"Well, then I'll send a little greeting," Syndrome sneered, and fired missiles at the plane.

Helen immediately saw the missiles approaching and jumped out of her seat. As the jet exploded, Elastigirl covered her kids with her outstretched body and then parachuted them safely down to the water.

Syndrome's computer confirmed the worst:

TARGET DESTROYED.

Mr. Incredible **SNAPPED**. He grabbed Mirage and
threatened to crush her unless Syndrome released him.
"Go ahead," Syndrome replied, calling his bluff.
But Mr. Incredible couldn't bring himself to hurt her.

Helen, Dash, and Vi made it to the island and hid in a cave to discuss their next move.

"Your father is in trouble," said Elastigirl. "I'm going to go look for him. Vi, you're in charge until I get back." She reached inside her duffel bag and pulled out three Super masks. "Put these on. Your identity is your most valuable possession. Protect it. If anything goes wrong, **USE YOUR POWERS**."

Dash was thrilled. He'd been waiting his entire life to use his super speed. But Violet was unsure. She hadn't yet mastered her powers and still lacked confidence.

After Helen left, Vi and Dash accidentally triggered an alarm. Syndrome's guards quickly responded. The Super kids defended themselves valiantly.

Dash **SPRINTED** through the jungle, ran over a cliff, and evaded multiple guards on velocipods. He even discovered that he could run on water!

Vi created a spherical **FORCE FIELD** around herself and her brother. Together they maneuvered the force field out of the island's brush, knocking down the bad guys.

Both Vi and Dash were relieved when their parents returned. Together the family fought Syndrome's goons, until . . .

. . . Syndrome himself suddenly appeared!

"**WHOA! WHOA! WHOA! TIME OUT!**" he yelled.

Within moments, the Incredible family was suspended in midair by the villain's immobi-ray! They were transported back to a prison chamber on Syndrome's base. He secured the heroes in suspension beams, then left to carry out his evil plan.

"This is my fault," Mr. Incredible said. "I swear I'm gonna get us out of this—"

But Violet was only half listening. She had already freed herself using her force field. She rolled over to the control panel, flipped a switch, and released her family.

The Incredibles knew they had to get off the island and save Municiberg from the Omnidroid. So they boarded one of Syndrome's rockets and blasted their way toward the mainland.

When they arrived, the city was in **CHAOS**.
Syndrome's plan had backfired. The Omnidroid
had outsmarted the villain and knocked him
unconscious. Thankfully, Frozone was there to help
the Incredibles battle the mechanical monster.

Bob remembered his first encounter with an
Omnidroid on Syndrome's island. "We can't stop
it!" he shouted. "The only thing hard enough to
penetrate it is . . . *ITSELF*!"

Bob grabbed one of the Omnidroid's claws. Helen used the remote control Syndrome had left behind to activate the rockets on the claw. Bob aimed the claw at the droid and released it. The claw blasted toward the Omnidroid and drilled right through the robot's body. The Omnidroid had been destroyed!

The crowd **CHEERED** for the Supers.

"Just like old times," Frozone whispered as all the heroes paused to enjoy the moment.

However, in all the excitement, Syndrome somehow disappeared!

The Incredibles found him waiting for them back at home. The villain grabbed baby Jack-Jack and flew through the roof toward his waiting jet.

Jack-Jack suddenly morphed into a **MINI MONSTER**! Terrified, Syndrome dropped the baby.

"Bob, throw me!" Helen shouted. She soared toward Jack-Jack and caught him in midair, then parachuted him safely to the ground.

Mr. Incredible launched his car toward the villain. Syndrome dodged the vehicle, but his long cape sucked him backward, directly into his jet's turbine!

The heroic family was **VICTORIOUS**, and Syndrome was never heard from again.

And so, the Incredibles returned to their **UNDERCOVER** life with a few alterations. Dash was allowed to join the track team— as long as he promised to never run too fast. And Vi had gained a bit more confidence after all her hero work. She mustered the courage to talk to her crush, Tony Rydinger, and even made plans to go to the movies with him.

The Parr family knew they could meet any challenge as long as they were **TOGETHER**. After all, the only thing stronger than a Super was a **FAMILY** of Supers!

INCREDIBLES 2

Adapted by **JESSICA COLBURN**

Illustrated by the **DISNEY STORYBOOK ART TEAM**

The Parr family was headed home after Dash's track meet when suddenly, the super villain known as the Underminer appeared! Using his tunneler, he burrowed deep beneath the city's largest bank. Once the bank collapsed into the chasm, the Underminer stole money from the vault.

Mr. Incredible tried to stop the Underminer, but the villain got away. Then the out-of-control tunneler breached the surface and hit the monorail tracks! Frozone quickly created an **ICE BRIDGE** to redirect the train and save the passengers.

The Incredibles worked fast to knock out the tunneler's engine. Finally, the machine stopped—just inches away from city hall.

But after they had saved the city from the runaway tunneler, the Incredibles were taken to the police station.

The police told Mr. Incredible and Elastigirl that Municiberg would have been better off if they had stayed away. The Supers had caused **EXTENSIVE DAMAGE** to the city and were responsible for letting the Underminer escape.

"So you support us . . . as long as we win?" asked Elastigirl.

The officer reminded Elastigirl that Superheroes were illegal. The police did not and would not support them.

Agent Rick Dicker from the National Supers Agency drove the Incredibles home after the interrogation. The family had been living in a motel since their house had been destroyed in a battle with a villain named Syndrome.

During the ride home, Violet revealed that her crush, Tony Rydinger, had seen her without her mask during the Underminer's attack. Rick said he would look into the Tony situation. He also had some bad news: his relocation division was being shut down. In two weeks, the family would be **ON THEIR OWN**—no home, no jobs, and **NO PROTECTION**.

At dinner that night, Violet and Dash argued with their parents. They wanted to keep fighting crime as a family. Helen **DISAGREED**.

"Superheroes are illegal. Whether it's fair or not, that's the law," she said.

Later that evening, Bob and Helen sat by the motel pool, trying to figure out what to do next.

Soon Lucius arrived. He told the Parrs that while they were being grilled by the police, he had been approached by a businessman who wanted to help make Supers legal.

"He wants to meet," said Lucius. **"TONIGHT!"**

With that, Bob and Helen changed into their old Supersuits, said goodbye to the kids, and headed with Lucius to **DEVTECH**, a massive telecommunications company.

"I love Superheroes!" said Winston Deavor, co-owner of DevTech.

Then he introduced his tech-genius sister, Evelyn. She explained that a small camera sewn into each Supersuit would record the Supers' heroic acts for everyone to see.

"It's about perception," Winston began. "You just be Super, and we'll get the public on your side. We won't stop until you're all legal again."

He offered the first mission to Elastigirl.

Back at the motel, Helen was conflicted about whether to take the job. "You know it's crazy, right?" she said. "To help my family, I've got to **LEAVE IT**; to fix the law, I've got to **BREAK IT**."

Bob reassured her that it would be good for all of them. He would take care of the kids while she was away.

Helen took a deep breath, picked up the phone, and called Winston to accept the assignment.

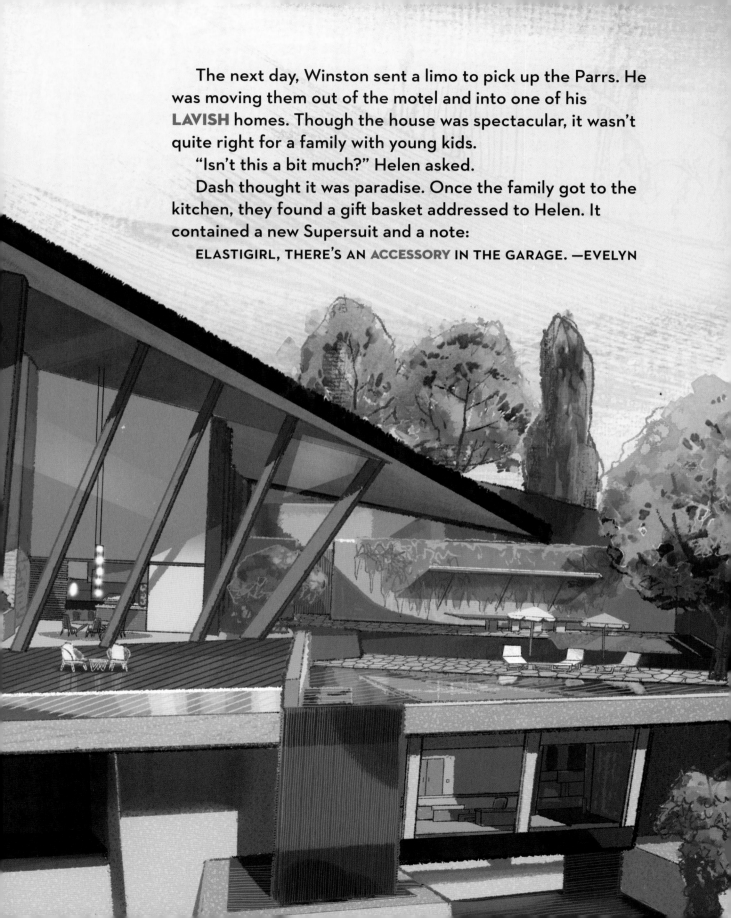

The next day, Winston sent a limo to pick up the Parrs. He was moving them out of the motel and into one of his LAVISH homes. Though the house was spectacular, it wasn't quite right for a family with young kids.

"Isn't this a bit much?" Helen asked.

Dash thought it was paradise. Once the family got to the kitchen, they found a gift basket addressed to Helen. It contained a new Supersuit and a note:

ELASTIGIRL, THERE'S AN ACCESSORY IN THE GARAGE. —EVELYN

The "accessory" was a jet-powered, all-electric
ELASTICYCLE! Helen jumped on the bike and
zoomed off to meet the Deavors at their private jet.
She soon learned that her first mission would be in
the sprawling city of New Urbem.

"You wanna make a big crime-fighting
statement, you go where the crime is big," said
Winston.

While Elastigirl worked with the Deavors to capture her acts of heroism on camera, Bob did his best to keep things running smoothly at home. That included negotiating a **CURFEW** with Violet before her date with Tony.

"Eleven-ish?" asked Violet.

"Ten-ish, heading for nine-thirty-ish!" Bob replied.

Bob also had to help Dash with his math **HOMEWORK**, which proved to be more difficult than he expected.

"Why would they change math? Math is math!" he yelled.

And then Bob needed to read
Jack-Jack a **BEDTIME STORY**.
  "'All over Doozle-Dorf, the Fribbers
of Frupp are going to sleep because
they just can't keep up.'" Bob began
to nod off himself . . . until Jack-Jack
gave him a gentle slap in the face.

Meanwhile, in New Urbem, Elastigirl was watching the ribbon-cutting ceremony at the new hovertrain station. But she had a strange feeling something was off.
Almost immediately, the hovertrain rose and raced out of the station . . . **BACKWARD!**

Elastigirl took off on her Elasticycle. She sped through tunnels, zoomed across rooftops, and finally leaped on top of the train. She stretched herself into a **PARACHUTE** to slow it down just moments before disaster.

The passengers were shaken but unharmed. The engineer stared blankly at Elastigirl. He had no idea what had happened.

Then a message appeared on the engineer's control panel: **WELCOME BACK, ELASTIGIRL. —THE SCREENSLAVER**

Back home, Bob was surprised to see Violet sitting by the door. Tony hadn't shown up for their date.

"Honey, why are you—?" Bob began.

Violet cut him off. **"DON'T SAY ANYTHING,"** she snapped, and stomped off to her room.

Just then, Bob realized that Jack-Jack had snuck out of his crib . . . again. Bob sat with the baby in front of the TV and eventually dozed off—but Jack-Jack was wide awake.

Outside the glass door, Jack-Jack saw a raccoon rummaging through the garbage. The Super baby approached the door—and phased through it! He was determined to confront the shady little critter.

Jack-Jack burst into **FLAMES**, threw patio furniture, and shot **LASER BEAMS** out of his eyes.

Bob rushed outside just as Jack-Jack multiplied himself and chased the raccoon away.

"You have powers!" he shouted. "Yeah, baby! And there's not a scratch on you."

But his excitement quickly waned. If Jack-Jack had uncontrollable powers, Bob was going to have a huge problem on his hands!

After Bob and Jack-Jack got settled back inside, Helen called to make sure everything was under control at home.

"Amazing as it may seem, it has been quite **UNEVENTFUL**," Bob lied. "How are you?"

Helen nearly burst with **EXCITEMENT**. "I saved a runaway train!" she exclaimed. "It was **SO GREAT**!"

Bob tried to be happy for her, but he was **JEALOUS**. He half listened to Helen while he flipped through the evening's news coverage. Every story centered on Elastigirl's daring rescue.

In bed that night, Bob tossed and turned. Helen was doing amazing work, and he could barely keep things afloat at home.

Meanwhile, Winston set up an exclusive TV interview for Elastigirl with anchorman Chad Brentley. But a few minutes into the program, a hypnotic pattern appeared on every screen in the studio.

The anchorman spoke in a robotic voice. "Screens are everywhere. We are controlled by screens. And screens are controlled by me, the Screenslaver!"

Elastigirl grabbed Chad to slap him out of his trance. Then the Screenslaver threatened to crash an ambassador's helicopter!

Elastigirl stretched out a window and climbed to the roof, where she saw three helicopters flying in formation. She launched herself toward the first one. There was no sign of the ambassador, but the pilots had been hypnotized! Elastigirl smashed the screens in the control panel to break their trance.

Elastigirl found the ambassador in the second helicopter. As the chopper spun out of control, she moved quickly to save the pilots. Then she **GRABBED** the ambassador, **SWUNG** out of the helicopter, and **LANDED** on the ground. The pilots of the third helicopter also managed to land. Everyone was safe!

The next morning, Violet was in a **FOUL MOOD**. She was upset with Tony for missing their date. And when she had confronted him at school, it had seemed he didn't know her at all. He acted like they had never met!

Bob understood what had happened—and tried to comfort Violet. "I can't tell you how many memories Dicker has had to erase over the years, when someone figured out your mother's or my identity—"

Violet couldn't believe her ears. **"IT WAS DICKER?"** she yelled. Then she scowled at her dad. "You told him about Tony. You had me erased from Tony's mind!" She grabbed her Supersuit and stuffed it into the **GARBAGE DISPOSAL**. "I hate Superheroes, and I renounce them!"

She turned on the disposal, but it was no use. The suit was indestructible. Violet screamed in frustration and stormed upstairs.

"Is she having adolescence?" Dash asked.

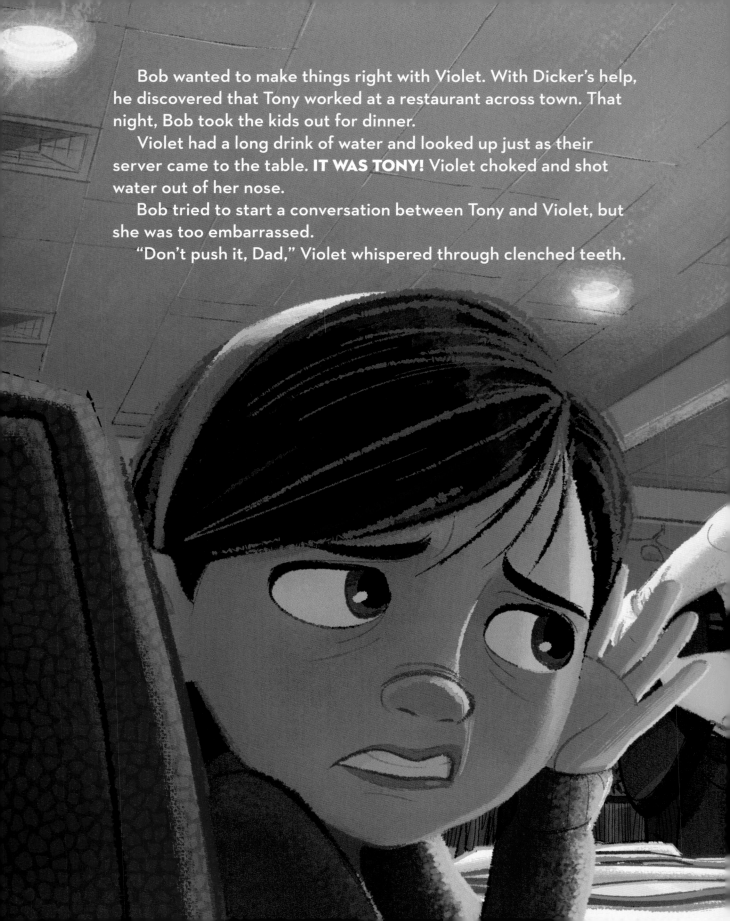

Bob wanted to make things right with Violet. With Dicker's help, he discovered that Tony worked at a restaurant across town. That night, Bob took the kids out for dinner.

Violet had a long drink of water and looked up just as their server came to the table. **IT WAS TONY!** Violet choked and shot water out of her nose.

Bob tried to start a conversation between Tony and Violet, but she was too embarrassed.

"Don't push it, Dad," Violet whispered through clenched teeth.

Meanwhile, Elastigirl used a tracking device created by Evelyn to pinpoint the Screenslaver's location. The tracker led Elastigirl to an apartment filled with hypnotizing equipment.

"Find anything interesting?" a voice asked menacingly. It was the Screenslaver!

Elastigirl chased him onto the roof, where, to her surprise, he jumped! She stretched herself into a parachute and held on to him as they fell. Suddenly, there was an **EXPLOSION**— the Screenslaver had destroyed the evidence in his lair.

When they landed, Elastigirl unmasked the Screenslaver to find a confused young man. He insisted he was innocent as the police dragged him away.

Back at home, Bob was frazzled—the kids were driving him crazy! To make matters worse, while watching TV with Dash, Bob saw his old Super car—THE INCREDIBILE— in the hands of a car collector.

"They told me it was destroyed!" he said to Dash.

Bob rummaged through some boxes and pulled out the Incredibile's remote control.

He pressed a button on it and the Incredibile's engine roared to life on the TV screen.

"WOW! IT WORKS?" exclaimed Dash as he snatched the remote and began pressing buttons.

Then Violet screamed as Jack-Jack, who'd **MORPHED** into a monster, chased her into the room. Violet and Dash were furious at Bob for not telling them about Jack-Jack's powers.

"I'm calling Lucius," Violet said.

When Lucius arrived, he watched in awe as Jack-Jack **DISAPPEARED** into another dimension.

"That is freaky!" said Lucius.

Bob was desperate, so he took Jack-Jack to the most inventive person he knew: 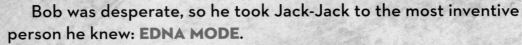 **EDNA MODE**.

"You look ghastly, Robert," she said when she saw him.

"I haven't been sleeping," replied Bob.

"Done properly, parenting is a heroic act," she began.

Bob tried to listen, but he was exhausted. He asked Edna if he could leave Jack-Jack with her for a while.

Edna was appalled. But then she saw that Jack-Jack was morphing, bit by bit, to look just like her. **"FASCINATING!"** she exclaimed. She decided she'd be happy to watch the baby. "Auntie Edna will take care of everything," she cooed to Jack-Jack.

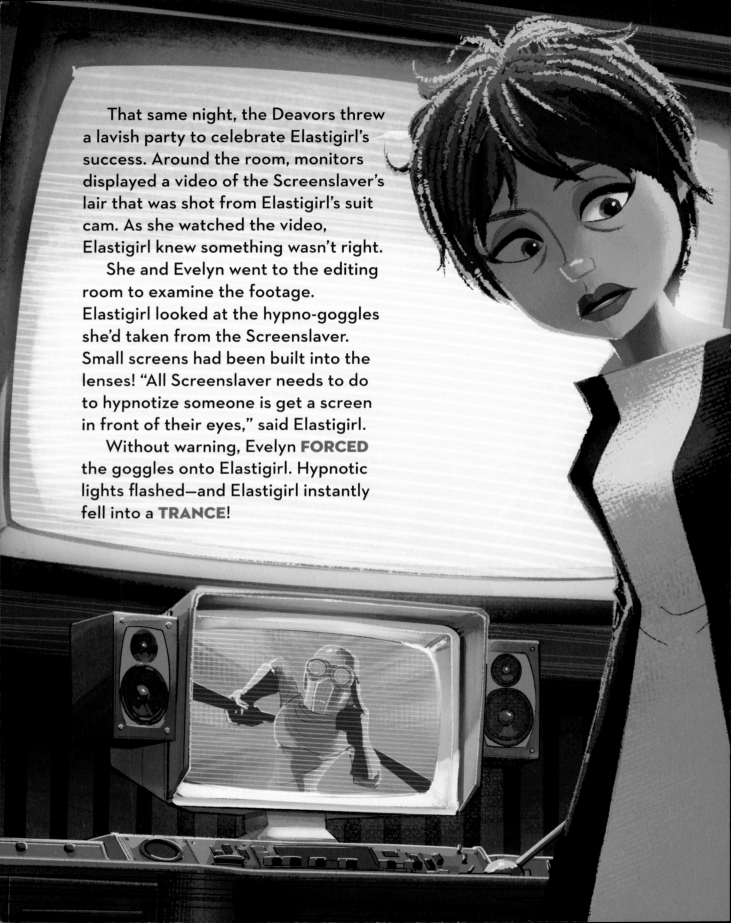

That same night, the Deavors threw a lavish party to celebrate Elastigirl's success. Around the room, monitors displayed a video of the Screenslaver's lair that was shot from Elastigirl's suit cam. As she watched the video, Elastigirl knew something wasn't right.

She and Evelyn went to the editing room to examine the footage. Elastigirl looked at the hypno-goggles she'd taken from the Screenslaver. Small screens had been built into the lenses! "All Screenslaver needs to do to hypnotize someone is get a screen in front of their eyes," said Elastigirl.

Without warning, Evelyn **FORCED** the goggles onto Elastigirl. Hypnotic lights flashed—and Elastigirl instantly fell into a **TRANCE!**

When Bob awoke the next morning, he was refreshed and recharged. He returned to Edna's and learned that she'd enjoyed watching Jack-Jack.

"He is pure unlimited potential," she said.

Edna had worked all night to perfect a Supersuit that could anticipate Jack-Jack's powers and send alerts to a tablet she'd designed. She put Jack-Jack in the testing chamber and handed Bob a **TRACKER**. She had planned for every outcome and **PROGRAMMED** the various solutions into the tracker.

Elastigirl was in need of serious help, too. Locked in a subzero computer room, she confronted Evelyn.

"So you're the Screenslaver," she said. "I counted on you!"

"That's why you failed," Evelyn sneered.

Evelyn had never wanted Supers to become legal. "Superheroes keep us **WEAK**," she explained. To trick everyone, she had hypnotized a pizza-delivery guy to play the Screenslaver. Not even Winston knew of her scheme.

"Are you going to kill me?" asked Elastigirl.

Evelyn smirked. "Nah, using you is better."

Bob took Jack-Jack home and showed Violet and Dash how to use Edna's tracker. Then he received a call from Evelyn.

"Elastigirl's in trouble. Meet me on the ship," she said.

Bob immediately called Lucius to watch the kids and left.

Soon after, six hypnotized Supers—all under Evelyn's control—arrived at the house and ordered the kids to go with them. Frozone appeared just in time to create a **GIANT WALL** of ice around the intruders. But the ice didn't hold them for long. A fight broke out. The hypnotized Supers were winning when suddenly, the Incredibile **CRASHED** into the living room. Dash had summoned it with the remote control! Frozone told the kids to get in and ordered the car to take them to safety. As the Incredibile sped away, the Supers slapped a pair of hypno-goggles on Frozone.

The kids knew their parents were in trouble. They told the
Incredibile to take them to the pier. But the ship had already left!
"Aww . . . I wish the Incredibile could follow that boat,"
groaned Dash.
The car **OBEYED** Dash's command: **HYDRO-PURSUIT ACTIVATED**.
The Incredibile sped off the pier, transformed into a water vehicle,
and zoomed after the ship.

The signing **CEREMONY** to make Supers legal again was about to begin. Delegates from around the world gathered in the conference room of Winston's state-of-the-art hydroliner.

The ambassador Elastigirl had saved from the helicopter was the first to sign the International Superhero Accord.

Violet, Dash, and Jack-Jack managed to use the Incredibile to board the ship. They fought their way past the hypnotized Supers and found their parents standing near the ship's damaged controls. Jack-Jack floated over to his mom and **REMOVED** her hypno-goggles.

Before long, all the Supers were freed from their trance.

Evelyn escaped in a jet that was hidden in the ship. With the help of a Super named Voyd, Elastigirl entered the cockpit. Evelyn sent the jet into a spinning climb as she **KICKED** Elastigirl. Without an oxygen mask, Elastigirl didn't have enough strength to fight back.

Back on the ship, the Supers realized they were on course to collide with the city. They had to work fast to turn the ship. While Mr. Incredible dove underwater to move the rudder, Frozone created icebergs to break off the hydrofoils.

Meanwhile, on the jet, Evelyn crashed through the windshield of the cockpit! Elastigirl leaped out and grabbed her as they both plummeted toward the ocean. Moments before they hit the water, Voyd caught the pair in a **PORTAL**. They fell through it and tumbled back onto the deck of the ship.

As the hydrofoils snapped, the ship turned and created a giant wave. Frozone transformed the wave into a snowbank, which acted as a **BARRIER** between the ship and the city. The hydroliner finally came to a stop. Everyone was safe, and the police **ARRESTED** the real Screenslaver.

Evelyn sneered at Elastigirl. "The fact that you saved me doesn't make you right," she said.

"But it does make you alive," Elastigirl replied.

The public was **GRATEFUL** to the Supers and saw them as heroes once more. Their legal status was officially restored!

A few days later, Violet reintroduced herself to Tony. The two finally went on their date, and the whole family decided to tag along.

On the way to the theater, police cars zoomed by with sirens blaring. Violet dropped Tony off and told him to save her a seat.

Then the Incredibles put on their masks, and their station wagon transformed into a new Incredibile. The Parrs would never be a normal family—but they were definitely a **SUPER** one!